POPULAR CULTURE

A VIEW FROM THE PAPARAZZI

Orlando Bloom	John Legend
Kelly Clarkson	Lindsay Lohan
Johnny Depp	Mandy Moore
Hilary Duff	Ashlee and Jessica Simpson
Will Ferrell	
Jake Gyllenhaal	Justin Timberlake
Paris and Nicky Hilton	Owen and Luke Wilson
LeBron James	Tiger Woods

Hilary Duff

Jim Whiting

Mason Crest Publishers

Hilary Duff

FRONTIS
Former "tween queen" Hilary Duff has starred in several hit movies and has sold more than 13 million albums in her brief career.

Produced by 21st Century Publishing and Communications, Inc.

Copyright © 2008 by Mason Crest Publishers. All rights reserved. No part of this publication may be reproduced or transmitted in any form or by any means, electronic or mechanical, including photocopying, recording, taping, or any information storage and retrieval system, without permission from the publisher.

MASON CREST PUBLISHERS INC.
370 Reed Road
Broomall, Pennsylvania 19008
(866) MCP-BOOK (toll free)
www.masoncrest.com

Printed in the United States.

First Printing

9 8 7 6 5 4 3 2 1

Library of Congress Cataloging-in-Publication Data

Whiting, Jim, 1943–
  Hilary Duff / Jim Whiting.
    p. cm. — (Pop culture: a view from the paparazzi)
  Includes bibliographical references and index.
  Hardback edition: ISBN-13: 978-1-4222-0201-2
  Paperback edition: ISBN-13: 978-1-4222-0355-2
  1. Actors—United State—Biography—Juvenile literature. 2. Duff, Hilary, 1987– —Juvenile literature. I. Title.
PN2287.D79W49 2008
792.02'8092—dc22
[B]
                                                                         2007020688

Publisher's notes:
- All quotations in this book come from original sources, and contain the spelling and grammatical inconsistencies of the original text.

- The Web sites mentioned in this book were active at the time of publication. The publisher is not responsible for Web sites that have changed their addresses or discontinued operation since the date of publication. The publisher will review and update the Web site addresses each time the book is reprinted.

CONTENTS

1	**A Star Is Born**	**7**
2	**Being Lizzie**	**13**
3	**A Time of Transformation**	**23**
4	**Ups and Downs**	**33**
5	**Moving Forward**	**45**
	Chronology	56
	Accomplishments & Awards	58
	Further Reading & Internet Resources	60
	Glossary	61
	Index	62
	Picture Credits	64
	About the Author	64

As a young girl, Hilary Duff dreamed of entertaining millions of people. Through years of hard work and disappointment, and with the support of her family, she was able to land the leading role in the Disney Channel television series *Lizzie McGuire*. The hit show would launch Hilary to stardom.

1

A Star Is Born

Many girls dream about becoming Hollywood stars. They dress up like their favorite actresses, spend countless hours on Internet fan sites, take dance lessons, and perform in school plays. A few especially brave ones may even ask their parents to take them to Hollywood when they get a little older.

When Haylie and Hilary Duff were growing up in Houston, Texas, during the 1990s, they had similar dreams of stardom. Unlike most other girls, however, the Duff sisters enjoyed a tiny taste of being in the limelight. Haylie won a small part in a 1996 made-for-TV movie called *Hope*. Hilary followed a year later with an appearance in another television movie, *True Women*.

The girls' experiences made them want more. Both movies were filmed in Texas, and they knew their home state was not exactly known for film production. The sisters urged their parents to let them go to Los Angeles and seek other acting jobs. Hilary later explained:

> "My sister and I knew that if we went to California we could go on real **auditions** for movies so we asked my parents and they were like 'It's a big step,' but they did it."

Their mother, Susan Duff, went with them. Robert "Bob" Duff, their dad, stayed behind to run the convenience store chain in which he was a partner. He flew out for visits whenever he could.

A Dose of Reality

It had been fairly easy for Haylie and Hilary to be noticed by entertainment professionals in Texas, because the number of talented young actors was somewhat limited. The Duffs soon found that this was not the case in Los Angeles. Hilary and her sister were competing for jobs with hundreds of young actors and it was hard to find work. At one point, the sisters had small parts in a television **pilot** called *The Underworld*, in which they were eaten by aliens.

They did not give up, though, and 1998 brought modest success. Haylie was cast in a movie called *Addams Family Reunion*, while Hilary played the heroine—a good witch who befriends Casper the Ghost—in the film *Casper Meets Wendy*. While making this film, Hilary had an amusing experience:

> "I was chasing after a goat for this one scene. The director screamed at me, 'Meaner, Meaner!' I ran faster with this angry expression on my face. The director yelled cut: 'Hilary, what are you doing?' he said. I told him I was just following directions. Turns out he was calling the goat—his name was Meaner."

A Star Is Born

Hilary began training for her career at an early age. "When we moved to San Antonio from Houston, we went to a performing arts school," she said. "We did a lot of plays and dances and stuff. My sister started doing it, so of course I had to start doing it—everything she does, I do!"

Starting to Get Noticed

Both films went straight to video and didn't attract much attention from movie critics. One of the few critics who noticed *Casper Meets Wendy* said, "Hilary Duff has a certain sparkle as Wendy," although another complained that she "spends the whole film grinning insanely." Hilary did receive a Young Artist Award nomination in the category of Best Performance in a TV Movie/Pilot/Mini-Series or Series–Young Actress Age Ten or Under, but she did not win.

The following year, Hilary earned a featured role in the made-for-TV movie *Soul Collector*, playing the daughter of a widow who is assisted by an angel. She received another young Artist Award nomination, for Best Performance in a TV Movie or Pilot—Supporting Young Actress, and this time she won. Hilary even won a small role in *Human*

Nature, a movie that premiered in 2001 at the prestigious Cannes Film Festival in France.

Delight and Disappointment

In 2000 Hilary finally got what she hoped would be a steady job when she was picked for a part on a new television series called *Daddio*. She would play one of the daughters of a salesman who stayed home to take care of the children while his attorney wife went back to work. "I had been on so many auditions and I finally got it. I was really excited," Hilary said.

The news got even better when Hilary learned that NBC had agreed to broadcast the show. This would be a huge opportunity, as

On *Lizzie McGuire*, Hilary was given some freedom to help create the role of Lizzie. "She certainly knows more about being a 13-year-old today than any of us," the show's producer, Stan Rogow, said. "And that's an example of how each and every one of these cast members is . . . bringing so much to his or her role."

she would be seen in millions of living rooms every week. She met the other cast members and enjoyed working with them to shoot the pilot. The star of the show, Michael Chiklis, later praised the young actor, saying:

> "After working with her the first day, I remember saying to my wife, 'This young girl is going to be a movie star.' She was completely at ease with herself and comfortable in her own skin."

Then the roof fell in. The producers of *Daddio* had decided to replace her in the television series. Hilary was crushed. She decided to go back to Texas and give up her dream of a show business career.

Reversal of Fortune

Two weeks later, Hilary got a surprise call from her manager. Executives who were producing a new television show for the Disney Channel wanted her to audition for a leading part. Hilary told her manager she was not interested, but Disney would not take "no" for an answer and she finally agreed to go.

The audition would change Hilary's life. She won the title role for a new Disney Channel show, *Lizzie McGuire*. Her talent and Disney's marketing genius would make *Lizzie* a huge hit. *Daddio*, meanwhile, was a flop that soon disappeared from the airwaves.

It turned out to be a good thing that *Daddio*'s producers had dumped Hilary. If they hadn't, she would not have been available for *Lizzie McGuire*, the series that made Hilary Duff a household name.

"When you're a kid, people don't necessarily give you credit for knowing what you want," Hilary has said. "But ever since I was little, even at six, I knew exactly what I wanted to do and what I wanted to be. I knew I wanted to work, and I knew I was willing to work hard to achieve my goals."

2

Being Lizzie

Hilary Erhard Duff was born in Houston on September 28, 1987. When she was growing up, she lived on a ranch outside of Austin, Texas, with her parents and sister Haylie, who is two years older than Hilary. The young singer and actress remembers her childhood as a pleasant time. She told authors Jill Rappaport and Wendy Wilkinson:

> "My parents used to put my older sister, Haylie, and me on the ponies when we were babies. We may have been just about able

> "to sit up, but we knew we had to hang on tight. I started riding at the age of four, and for the next several years Haylie and I were lucky enough to have two Shetland ponies and a Welsh."

From a young age, Hilary and Haylie loved to perform together. "We would play in our bedrooms every single night together, act out scenes that we saw in movies, play dress up together and act like we were someone else," Hilary recalled.

They found a larger stage when Haylie began taking ballet lessons. Hilary didn't want to be left behind, so she soon started lessons as well. It did not take long to prove her ability. In 1993, the BalletMet of Columbus, Ohio, went on tour to perform the traditional Christmas ballet *Nutcracker*. It is far too expensive for professional companies to bring along the dozens of child dancers that the *Nutcracker* requires when they travel. So the BalletMet put out a casting call for children in the areas where it was performing, including Texas.

Winning a spot in the *Nutcracker* would not be easy. The young dancers would have to be fast learners, because they would not have much time to rehearse. They would also have to be very talented. Six-year-old Hilary obviously measured up, as she was selected to join the company. It was her stage debut.

Acting Career

Haylie soon decided to give up ballet for acting. However, Hilary was a little reluctant to take this new direction at first. She explained to Lynn Barker of *Teen Television*:

> "My sister was doing a Romeo and Juliet Shakespeare play and she didn't want to be bad in front of her friends because she had a lead part so there was a little acting workshop near our house and she started to go and my mom asked me if I wanted to go and I thought 'Oh, that's so stupid. I would never want to do that.'"

It didn't take long for Hilary to have a change of heart. "My sister kept coming home showing me all this stuff and I was 'mom, I want to do that,'" she continued. "So I just kind of followed in her footsteps."

Being Lizzie 15

Haylie Duff poses with her little sister at a 2004 fashion show in Los Angeles. The sisters have always had a close relationship, and Haylie has supported Hilary while also pursuing her own career. "My sister and I are best friends and we get along so well," Hilary says. "She is so talented and inspiring to me."

Their early work at the acting workshop led to Haylie and Hilary's appearances in the television movies *Hope* and *True Women*.

Some parents who see a spark of talent in their young children become notorious "stage mothers," aggressively pushing their kids toward show business. This was not the case with the Duff family. Instead, the **impetus** came from Haylie and Hilary. However, Bob and Susan Duff were willing to support their children's dreams of acting careers. As reporter Kate Stroup wrote in a *Newsweek* article about Hilary:

> "When the kids begged to be performers, [Susan Duff] loaded them all into the family Acura—along with a hermit crab, a gerbil, two goldfish and a rabbit—and drove the 20 hours from Austin to L.A."

A Bad Beginning

Their welcome to Los Angeles was anything but warm. Susan Duff had paid someone $1,000 to set up auditions for Haylie and Hilary, but the person disappeared with their money. Many people would have given up and gone home, but the Duffs decided to keep trying. Hilary later explained:

> "My mom went to this bookstore and she got all these books on the business and what to do and how to get an agent. She worked super hard for us and she got us an agent and a manager and a couple of auditions."

A couple of auditions quickly turned into many more. Virtually all of them ended in failure. It was tiring and discouraging. "[We were] going to audition after audition after audition," Haylie explained. "You can go on 500 auditions and maybe get two **callbacks**."

Facing Stiff Competition

When executive producer Stan Rogow was looking for someone to play the character of Lizzie McGuire for a new Disney television series, he and the show's other creators considered thousands of young actresses. Rogow was looking for an "average girl"—a character who did not fit into a simple **stereotype**, such as cheerleader, diva, or jock. In addition to Hilary, many other young actresses—including Lindsay Lohan and Sara Paxton—were given serious consideration for the part. The group was eventually narrowed to three, and Hilary was finally chosen. Rogow later told Fred Shuster of the *Daily News of Los Angeles*:

> **"Each time we saw Hilary, she was more interesting to watch. So, while the auditioning process can be painful, part of what's revealed is who you're not getting bored with. Slowly, you began not to be able to take your eyes off Hilary. It became, 'That's the girl.'"**

Somewhat humorously, Disney Channel executive Rich Ross offered another explanation for Hilary's selection. "We called her in four times," he said. "She wasn't doing anything wrong. She just wore such great outfits, and we wanted to see what she'd come in with next."

At first, the producers called their new show *What's Lizzie Thinking*. To make sure the audience would know just what Lizzie was thinking,

A group of Disney executives, including *Lizzie McGuire* producer Stan Rogow (right), are photographed at the premiere of *The Lizzie McGuire Movie* in April 2003. Three years earlier Rogow had chosen 12-year-old Hilary from the thousands of young actresses hoping to get the lead part in the Disney Channel series.

they included a cartoon character named "Animated Lizzie" to say Lizzie's thoughts out loud. In addition to playing Lizzie on-screen, Hilary also provided the voice for Animated Lizzie.

Making Lizzie

By the time the show began production, Disney had changed the name of the series to *Lizzie McGuire*. The show was about the

The Animated Lizzie cartoon leans on Hilary's arm in this promotional photo from *Lizzie McGuire*. "I think we're totally alike in our clothes, makeup, and hair," Hilary said of her television character. "I think she's a little more insecure." First aired in January 2001, the series soon became one of the Disney Channel's biggest hits.

everyday experiences of an awkward and self-conscious seventh grader who must deal with the typical problems of adolescence. As Hilary explained to Laura Girardi of *Time for Kids*:

> "Lizzie's really insecure. She's not comfortable with herself. She doesn't know who she is. I think that's also why so many people relate to the show: She's just trying to find herself, like any other 14- or 15-year-old girl."

Hilary had to work hard so the show would be ready for its premiere early in 2001. Because of the demands of making a television show, she did not have time to go to school. A tutor was hired to help Hilary with her lessons when she was not on camera.

In the series Lizzie has two close friends, Miranda and Gordo. Lalaine Vergara-Paras, a young actress whom Hilary already knew, was cast as Miranda, while Adam Lamberg played Gordo. Veteran actors Hallie Todd and Robert Carradine were hired to play her parents, while Jake Thomas portrayed Lizzie's younger brother Matt.

The first episode, entitled "Rumors," aired on January 19, 2001. *Lizzie McGuire* was an immediate hit, with the highest-rated premiere of any original Disney Channel program. It soon became the network's most popular show, with a weekly audience of several million viewers.

Broad Appeal

The program's popularity was easy to understand. The character of Lizzie appealed to young viewers, especially girls. They identified with Lizzie's struggle to be a good friend, her relationships with her parents and annoying younger brother, her growing interest in cute boys, and her conflicts with rival girls like Kate Saunders, the most popular girl in the school. The filming was creative and interesting, and many shows managed to be funny and serious at the same time.

The primary audience was **tweens**, girls between the ages of eight and twelve. However, young girls weren't the only ones who enjoyed *Lizzie McGuire*. Many of their mothers also watched the show, and even some young women in the 20s admitted to being fans. Hilary explained:

HILARY DUFF

> **"It's got something for everyone. Girls like it because it's about them. Parents come up to me all the time and say they love it because it reflects their kids. The characters are easy to relate to."**

For Hilary, the show had another benefit besides creating instant stardom and recognizability. A singer named Aaron Carter appeared in one of the early episodes. Even though he was several months younger than Hilary, he had already released three albums and had a string of hit singles, so he was famous enough to play himself on the show. Hilary and Aaron hit it off and soon began dating.

A Marketing Phenomenon

As *Lizzie McGuire* took off with tweens and teens and became the highest-rated program in its time slot, the formidable Disney marketing machine went to work. By August 2002 the company was collaborating with a clothing firm called Limited Too to produce a line of Lizzie outfits for tweens and teens. The show also generated a line of accessories for young girls, several dolls, and a series of graphic novels based on original episodes. Within a year, the *Wall Street Journal* reported that Disney had made nearly $100 million on Lizzie McGuire merchandise.

Disney also cashed in on Hilary's fame by casting her in *Cadet Kelly*, a made-for-TV movie that aired early in 2002 on the Disney Channel. *Cadet Kelly* became the most watched program in the network's history. Hilary played Kelly Collins, a 14-year-old girl who is used to having her freedom. When her divorced mother marries the commandant of a military academy, Kelly has to attend the school and get used to its strict discipline. Critic Aaron Wallace commented:

> **"Instead of the decidedly stereotypical 'teen girl' performance that she gives—with a certain charm, I might add—in *Lizzie McGuire* and so many of her movies, her character here is much more aloof. Duff's portrayal of a free spirit with conviction is believable and shows off just a bit more acting talent than some may realize that she has."**

To cash in on the popularity of *Lizzie McGuire*, Disney began to sell many items branded with the image of Lizzie or Hilary, including clothing, graphic novels, and fashion accessories for young girls. These Hilary Duff dolls—showing her as a pop star, movie star, and television star—were available in toy stores in 2003.

All Good Things Must End

Hilary worked on *Lizzie McGuire* through the summer of 2002. The show was such a hit that Disney ordered additional episodes to be filmed. Her sister Haylie even appeared in several episodes, as the cousin of mean girl Kate Saunders. But once 65 episodes had been finished, Disney decided to end the series. This was a longstanding policy of the company: 65 episodes was the minimum needed for **syndication**, and Disney executives felt that the writing of a series would become stale if it were permitted to continue beyond that point.

This did not necessarily mean the end of the Lizzie character, however. In late 2002 the ABC network, which is owned by Disney, began planning a new series about Lizzie as a high school student. However, Disney and the Duffs could not agree on how much Hilary should be paid. She had earned about $15,000 an episode for *Lizzie McGuire*. Unconfirmed reports indicated that Disney had offered $35,000 per episode for the new series, while Susan Duff had asked for $100,000 per episode. There were other areas of conflict as well. Annoyed at what they called Disney's "bullying," the Duffs eventually decided to leave Disney. The last episode of *Lizzie McGuire* aired in 2004.

"I loved working on *Lizzie McGuire*," Hilary told an interviewer shortly after Disney cancelled the television series. "I worked every day for two years and when you work every day on something, it can get kind of tiring, but I loved the cast and crew . . . they were amazing."

3
A Time of Transformation

Hilary's fans were disappointed to learn that she would no longer be playing Lizzie McGuire on television. For Hilary, however, 2003 was an exciting year. By the end of the year she would transform herself into a star with international appeal, expanding into big-screen movies and beginning a career as a singer.

On the Big Screen

During the spring of 2003, Hilary starred in two films. The first was *Agent Cody Banks*, which featured her friend Frankie Muniz, star of the television series *Malcolm in the*

Middle. The movie was a spoof of spy films, with plenty of high-tech gizmos, dastardly villains, lots of action, and daring rescues. As a result, it included numerous jokes for people familiar with spies and their history. For example, Natalie (the name of Hilary's character) and Cody attend the fictitious William Donovan Preparatory School. The real-life William Donovan was the director of the World War II–era Office of Strategic Services, the predecessor of today's Central Intelligence Agency (CIA).

In one scene, the script called for Hilary and Frankie to kiss. She told Lynn Barker:

> "It was really weird. We had kissed on *Lizzie McGuire* before. There were so many people watching that it was kind of embarrassing."

Because there were so many young people who were fans of Hilary and Frankie, *Agent Cody Banks* did well at the box office. The young stars drew praise for their acting from movie critics. Josh Bell of *Las Vegas Weekly* noted that "Muniz and Duff are cute and charismatic." David Noh of *Film Journal International* said, "TV favorite Muniz has a bright, underdog charm," while "Duff has a sweet-yet-strong quality." Others singled out Muniz—which was not too surprising, since he played the title character. Robert Roten of the *Laramie Movie Scope* commented, "Most of the film's charm lies in Banks' awkwardness around girls, and his clumsy attempts to show Natalie that he is not the clueless dork he seems to be."

In the Spotlight

Of course Hilary had the leading role in *The Lizzie McGuire Movie*, which opened several weeks after *Agent Cody Banks*. The film depicted Lizzie's adventures after graduating from junior high school and taking a trip with her class to Rome. Hilary faced the challenge of playing two different parts: In addition to Lizzie, she plays an Italian singer named Isabella who is a dead ringer for Lizzie.

Hilary's fans flocked to theatres when *The Lizzie McGuire Movie* opened, and the film made $17 million in its first weekend. It was a surprise hit, eventually earning more than $50 million for Disney. Movie critic Eleanor Ringel Gillespie of the *Atlanta Journal-Constitution* identified the film's appeal:

A Time of Transformation

> "Adolescent girls will love watching Hilary do her thing. *The Lizzie McGuire Movie* is a cute teen movie, starring a cute teen idol, who stars in her own cute teen TV series, which provides the basis for this cute teen movie.... Duff is very appealing."

Her appeal was obvious when the Teen Choice Awards were announced. Hilary won in the Choice Movie Breakout Star—Female category and received two additional nominations: Choice Movie—Comedy and Choice Movie Actress—Comedy.

Hilary capped the year with an appearance in a third film, *Cheaper by the Dozen*, which opened the day after Christmas. Although the film did very well at the box office, earning more than $190 million, critical

Hilary had originally met her *Agent Cody Banks* costar Frankie Muniz when he appeared on an episode of *Lizzie McGuire*. Although the two were rumored to be dating, Hilary maintained that they were only friends. Hilary earned $500,000 for playing the role of Natalie in *Agent Cody Banks*, and doubled that paycheck to $1 million for *The Lizzie McGuire Movie*.

opinion was lukewarm. Most of the focus was on the film's main stars, Steve Martin, Bonnie Hunt, and Ashton Kutcher. Hilary's role as one of twelve siblings did not attract much notice.

A Public Feud

By that time Hilary's life had undergone another change. She had already discovered one of the downsides of being famous—her relationship with Aaron Carter had been frequently discussed in tabloids, magazines, and gossip columns. She and Aaron broke up after Aaron admitted that he had cheated on her.

The breakup attracted even more attention. It led to a feud between Hilary and Lindsay Lohan, who had dated Aaron before Hilary. The two stars traded nasty comments in the media and snubbed each other

A poster for *The Lizzie McGuire Movie*, which surprised many people by becoming a big hit at the box office. Hilary enjoyed making the movie, and received praise from director Jim Hunt. "She was a complete professional," he said. "She was able to do exactly what was expected so quickly and so naturally."

A Time of Transformation

In 2003 and 2004 a feud developed between Hilary and another Disney star, actress Lindsay Lohan. (Both are pictured on the July 2003 *Vanity Fair* cover: Hilary is in the center and Lindsay is on the right). The two celebrities traded nasty comments after singer Aaron Carter broke up with Lindsay to date Hilary.

at movie premieres and other public events. Duff called the feud "silly," and eventually she and Lindsay patched up their differences.

Getting Started in Music

Perhaps the biggest change in Hilary's life during 2003 was becoming a pop star. Apart from singing in her church choir, Hilary had virtually no musical background when she came to California. The "music bug" bit Hilary in the summer of 2001 at a Radio Disney concert in Anaheim, California, she later admitted to Craig Rosen of *Billboard* magazine:

> "There were all these pop acts backstage at the concert. They were all getting ready backstage and warming up, and I was like, 'I want to do this so bad.'"

Help was literally only a few feet away in the form of Andre Recke, a well-known music manager who became acquainted with Hilary at the concert. "When I met Hilary, I knew she had something special," he told Rosen. "Sometimes you just have that feeling, that, 'Wow, she's a star.'" Music industry executives like Jay Landers of Walt Disney Records agreed. Landers explained:

> "There are singers like Barbra Streisand, Celine Dion and Whitney Houston, who have legendary voices. There are artists like Britney Spears with lesser voices, yet they have the ability to communicate. They all possess that unique thing we call **charisma**. From the moment we met Hilary, it was evident that she has that in abundance."

Hilary, her mom, and Recke agreed that she should not rush into recording. First she had to take singing lessons. A year later, Hilary recorded the song "I Can't Wait" for the *Lizzie McGuire* soundtrack album, and the song became a minor hit. The next step was a Christmas album, *Santa Claus Lane*. Released late in 2002, it was a combination of popular Christmas music and some original songs. Aided by a tie-in with the movie *The Santa Clause 2*, *Santa Claus Lane* eventually sold more than 500,000 copies.

Triple Threat

With these experiences under her belt, Hilary was ready to record a full-length album of new material. The title of the album, *Metamorphosis*, reflected the many changes that were occurring in Hilary's life and career. She told *Canada AM*'s Seamus O'Regan:

> "I think a lot of people knew me as characters that I've played on TV or in movies and I wanted them to get to know more about Hilary. So, we decided to call [the album] *Metamorphosis*."

Metamorphosis enjoyed brisk sales from the moment it was released on August 26, 2003. It quickly soared to the top of the Billboard charts and went double **platinum** by the end of the year (meaning it sold at least 2 million copies). Total sales of *Metamorphosis* eventually reached

A Time of Transformation 29

Hilary takes a break in a recording studio, 2003. In an interview on the DVD *Hilary Duff: All Access Pass*, she explained, "When you're singing in the studio, it's all about you. It's really personal." Hilary's first recording success came with the song "I Can't Wait," which was included on a *Lizzie McGuire* soundtrack album.

Hilary appears on the cover of *Fashion* magazine's fall 2003 issue. The success of her album *Metamorphosis*, as well as Hilary's hit movies and the continuing appeal of *Lizzie McGuire* (which continued to run on the Disney Channel through 2004) made her one of the hottest young stars of the year.

nearly 4 million. The album's first single, "So Yesterday," was number one on Billboard's Hot 100 for two weeks.

In a *USA Today* article, Brian Mansfield explained how marketing executives at Disney had cleverly used Hilary's popularity as an actress to make her debut album a hit. He wrote:

> "Hilary Duff became the first of what [Disney Channel executive in charge of music Stephen] Vincent likes to call 'The Triple Threat Kids'—young stars who can act and sing and have at least one other talent. . . . Disney used Duff's series, *Lizzie McGuire*, and a feature film to set the stage for her singing career."

Rave Reviews

A number of music reviewers had good things to say about the album. Stephen Thomas Erlewine of the publication *All Music Guide* wrote:

> "Hilary Duff's debut, *Metamorphosis*, is what teen pop *should* sound like in 2003. It picks up on mainstream trends . . . but turns them light and sweet, making for a very good modern bubblegum album. One of the keys to its success is that Duff is never sexed up, the way that Britney Spears was right from the start of her career. . . . *Metamorphosis* is the musical equivalent of *Lizzie McGuire*, only splashier and savvier."

The album's success paved the way for Hilary to perform at the American Music Awards in November 2003. It had been just over two years since she had stood backstage at the Radio Disney concert in Anaheim, envying the performers as they warmed up. Now she was performing in front of the music industry's biggest stars while millions of people watched her on television. Not surprisingly she was a little nervous, but she did just fine. Soon afterward Hilary began her Metamorphosis Club Tour, appearing live in concert before her fans.

Truly, 2003 had been a remarkable year.

Hilary was pleased by her ascent to stardom, but despite all of the media hype she tried to keep a level head. "It's all a big blur," the teenaged singer and actor told *Popstar!* magazine in 2004. "Even though [my success] didn't happen fast—it happened in four years—it's kind of weird."

4
Ups and Downs

Hilary expanded into the fashion world in March 2004 with the launch of her personalized clothing line, Stuff by Hilary Duff. The new label emphasized leisure wear such as T-shirts, track suits, and dark denim skirts. Soon it would branch out to include school supplies, accessories, and even a fragrance.

Stuff by Hilary Duff also reflected Hilary's personal values. As she explained when the line was shown for the first time:

> "Looking good and being trendy shouldn't mean showing off a lot of skin. The clothes can let girls be creative and have fun fashions without being super revealing. . . . I hope that they don't wear a low-cut shirt to try and get a guy, because that definitely wouldn't be the way to go about doing it."

A few weeks afterward, Hilary won the Kids' Choice Award for Favorite Female Singer for *Metamorphosis*. Later that year she would be named Best New Female Artist at the World Music Awards. She was also nominated for a Juno Award (Canada's version of the Grammys) and an MTV Video Music Award.

Smashing the Glass Slipper

Her movie career continued with the release of *A Cinderella Story* in July 2004. Hilary relished the opportunity to do a modern version of the classic fairy tale, with Chad Michael Murray as a contemporary Prince Charming. Updates included the substitution of a missing cell phone for the traditional glass slipper. As she told Lynn Barker:

> "It's a totally different character than I've ever played . . . The *Cinderella Story* is different. She's very independent. She's a plain Jane and she has a metamorphosis. I'm hoping it will appeal to a bit older audience."

Movie critics didn't share Hilary's opinion, and she received her first negative reviews. Winda Benedetti of the *Seattle Post-Intelligencer* headlined her review "'Cinderella Story' takes a promising premise and lays a big fat pumpkin," and said of Hilary that "she's cute but . . . not particularly interesting to watch." Thomas Delapa of *Boulder Weekly* added, "This retread fairy tale is anything but charming. The only thing missing is the pumpkin that turns into a coach. That's OK, because Duff turns into a turkey way before midnight." And Tyler Hanley of *Palo Alto Weekly* said "Duff is a let-down. . . . Her acting feels stilted and . . . superficial."

John Monaghan of the *Detroit Free Press* termed Hilary "likable" and "nearly irresistible to watch." But he added, "The movie is a step down for Duff, who owes her fans and herself something fresher than another lazy **rehash** of the world's most-exploited fairy tale."

Golden Girl

Hilary's name on the **marquee** proved to be stronger than the negative opinions. The film was a hit, earning more than $50 million at the box office. According to Nick Duerden of *Blender*:

> "She essentially plays an extension of herself, a sweet wholesome girl who shuns the very notion of bad behavior and instead exemplifies the benefits of a decent upbringing. In short, the characters she plays—and Hilary herself—are the kind of daughter every mom would want. All of which combines to make her box office gold."

At about the same time that the movie came out, Hilary confirmed what many people had suspected for several months. She and Joel Madden, singer for the alternative rock band Good Charlotte, were an item. In view of her public image as a clean-cut role model for

Teen heartthrob Chad Michael Murray (right) speaks to Hilary in a scene from *A Cinderella Story*. "He's really cool. He's so down-to-earth and so nice and a really cool guy," Hilary said of her costar. When *A Cinderella Story* was released in mid-2004, it proved to be a hit among Hilary's young fans.

HILARY DUFF

Joel Madden, singer and guitarist for the punk rock band Good Charlotte, walks with Hilary and a pet dog. The two began dating in 2004, even though the tattooed Madden was eight years older. "I'm really happy right now," she told MTV in July 2005, when news of the relationship became public. "I feel really lucky to have him."

young girls, Madden seemed an odd choice. Not only was he eight years older than Hilary, he also sported a number of tattoos. To Hilary, the tattoos were no big deal. "After two months, I didn't even see his tattoos anymore, because that's not who he is," she told Lori Berger of *CosmoGIRL*.

Hilary spent most of the second half of 2004 on a sold-out tour to promote her second album, *Hilary Duff*. The album was released on her birthday, September 28. One reason for naming it after herself was that Hilary had a much higher degree of direct involvement in making the album than she had on her first record. She felt that *Hilary Duff* was more personal than *Metamorphosis* had been.

Although *Hilary Duff* debuted at number two on the Billboard 200 and was eventually certified platinum, its total sales were lower than the sales for *Metamorphosis*. In general, it was not as well received as *Metamorphosis* had been, and some reviewers compared Hilary unfavorably with pop stars like Avril Lavigne and Ashlee Simpson. On the other hand, *All Music Guide*'s Stephen Erlewine noted:

> "It might take itself a little seriously, it might be a little uneven, but [*Hilary Duff*] feels like the soundtrack to the life of a smart, ambitious, popular teenager trying to sort things out."

Raise Your Voice

Hilary's acting took a more serious turn in *Raise Your Voice*, which was released to theaters in October 2004. She played Terri Fletcher, whose dreams of a singing career are put on hold after her brother's tragic death, in part because of her father's opposition. Aided by an encouraging music professor, played by John Corbett, Terri is able to overcome the obstacles.

Corbett liked Hilary's work. "She moved me in this movie," he said. "When I saw her being so raw and open—they got really good stuff on her—and when she started crying in this movie, I started crying." Anita Gates of the *New York Times* also thought highly of Hilary, writing:

> "Duff's screen presence and the film's infectious high spirits will make this piece of fluff appealing to young moviegoers without conveying any sinister messages."

HILARY DUFF

Hilary (center) is pictured with the other cast members of *Raise Your Voice* in this poster. The film was a box office flop and most reviewers were critical, although a few praised Hilary's performance. "Ms. Duff's screen presence ... will make this piece of fluff appealing to young moviegoers," wrote Anita Gates in the *New York Times*.

However, most critics did not like the film, and this time her fans seemed to agree. The film made slightly over $10 million, less than a fifth of what *A Cinderella Story* had taken in. Perhaps the worst cut of all came from the Golden Raspberry Foundation, which each year gives dubious "awards" known as Razzies to those films and actors they consider the worst of each year. Hilary was nominated as Worst Actress for both *A Cinderella Story* and *Raise Your Voice*.

Not Quite Perfect

Hilary's next film project was *The Perfect Man*, which was released in June 2005. Her character, Holly, is tired of seeing her mother (played by Heather Locklear) in one relationship after another with losers. She decides that her mother needs a perfect man. Since no perfect man actually exists, Holly creates one using the Internet.

Ups and Downs 39

A fashionable Hilary appears on the cover of *Teen Vogue*, 2004. That year Hilary launched her clothing line for tweens, Stuff by Hilary Duff. The line has been a huge success, with annual sales expected to increase to more than $200 million over the next few years as Stuff becomes available at more retail outlets.

The movie was a modest hit, earning about $19 million, but it was not as successful as the producers had hoped it might be. Although many critics disliked the movie, a few found good things to say about Hilary's performance. Nancy Churnin of the *Dallas Morning News* wrote:

> "*The Perfect Man* is not the perfect movie, but it sports some very appealing moments.... Ms. Duff projects so much appeal that she leaps over lapses in logic like Super Mario over lava pits."

As for Hilary, she shrugged off the criticism, telling the *New York Times* that as long as her fans liked her work, she didn't care what people wrote. She said:

> "The 50-year-old person that's writing the review is not who is meant to see my movie. I don't care what they think of the movie. They're 50. They're not the **demographic**."

Hilary bounced back in August 2005 when her third album, *Most Wanted*, was released. It was a combination of some of her earlier songs, **remixes**, and several new tracks that Joel Madden and his twin brother Benji had helped her to record. *Most Wanted* lived up to its name by selling more than 200,000 copies in its first week and reaching number one on the Billboard 200 chart. It was certified platinum by the end of September.

Hilary Helps Out

In August 2005 a major storm, Hurricane Katrina, pounded the Gulf coast of the United States, leaving millions of people homeless in New Orleans and other communities and causing billions of dollars in damage. Hilary quickly stepped up to help the victims of the disaster, donating $250,000 to relief efforts. She also encouraged fans to bring canned goods to her concerts, and had the food and other items sent to help those in need.

Hilary has a long commitment to charitable giving. In 1999 she became involved with Kids with a Cause, an organization that helps disadvantaged youngsters in the United States and overseas. Hilary and

Ups and Downs

"I don't know exactly how to explain what we're doing, but it's fun and funky and different, something new for me. It's really cool," Hilary told MTV while recording her third studio album, *Most Wanted*. The album was Hilary's second to hit number one on the Billboard charts, and eventually sold more than 1.3 million copies in the United States.

HILARY DUFF

As her career has taken off, Hilary has been very involved with a number of charitable organizations. Here, she reads to the children of U.S. soldiers during an event on Capitol Hill, June 2005. The event was held to help kick off National Military Families Week to recognize the importance of military families.

her sister Haylie do more than just donate money and lead fundraising efforts. They also give their time, visiting hospitals and painting with the youngsters confined there. When a catastrophic **tsunami** struck Indonesia late in 2004, Hilary donated a significant portion of ticket sales from her Most Wanted tour to Kids with a Cause to ease the suffering in that country. She explained:

> "I, just like everyone else, have watched this terrible tragedy and feel so sorry for the children and the families who have lost so much. I want to do everything I can to help those that have survived."

Hilary is also active in the Lance Armstrong Foundation (which provides support for people with cancer), the Toy Mountain Campaign (which gathers toys during the holiday season), USA Harvest (which collects surplus food and distributes it to homeless shelters and similar outlets), and several other charitable groups.

Perhaps the charity closest to her heart harks back to the days when she was riding horses on the family's ranch. The organization Return to Freedom protects wild horses to keep them from being slaughtered. She served as the organization's youth ambassador from 2003 to 2005.

Another Episode of *Cheaper*

At the end of the year, Hilary appeared in *Cheaper by the Dozen 2*, released during the holiday season. The plot involved competition between her family and another one. Randy Cordova of the *Arizona Republic* was virtually alone among critics in noting that "it aims to be pleasant and good-natured, which it is. There are enough laughs scattered throughout to keep everything moderately amusing, and the cast is likeable." Virtually everyone else panned the film, and a few singled out Hilary for criticism. However, *Cheaper by the Dozen 2* was another big hit, earning more than $129 million at the box office.

As she grows older, Hilary's career direction has reflected the changes in her life. In 2007 she appeared in *War, Inc.*, a black comedy that was much different from her earlier film roles. Many listeners and music critics agreed that her 2007 album *Dignity* also reflected her development as a recording artist.

5

Moving Forward

Because she is involved in so many projects, it is not surprising that Hilary Duff earns a lot of money. In April 2006, *Forbes* magazine reported that the 19-year-old had earned $15 million during the previous year, ranking Hilary fourth among people under the age of 25 (professional basketball star LeBron James topped the list at $22.9 million).

One of her more interesting projects of 2006 was working with the toy company Mattel to create a new line of Barbie dolls. "I designed, like, five outfits for it, and it has a Hilary face," she told *Blender*. "And to get the proportions right, they did this thing where you stand in a machine and they digitally scan your body."

In August 2006 Hilary's film *Material Girls* was released. Making the film was an opportunity to work with her family: Haylie was the costar and Susan Duff served as one of the producers. The sisters played cosmetic company heiresses who try to save their company from bankruptcy.

Box-Office Disappointment

Unfortunately, ominous signs swirled about *Material Girls* almost from the beginning. After filming was completed, there were rumors that the movie was so bad that it would never be released to theaters, and it did take longer than normal for the film to find a distributor. Although *Material Girls* did eventually appear in theaters, it did not do very well, bringing in just $11 million. This was only slightly more than it had cost to make the film.

Most critics detested the film, with Eric Lurio of *Entertainment Insiders* writing, "*Material Girls* is a dumb film." Though Pam Grady of *Reel Review* commented that "There is no edge to the movie at all, and that blandness will render it forgettable to anyone over the age of 12 or so," she added:

> "[*Material Girls*] is pleasant enough, and occasionally even fun.... Not that the Duff sisters or director Martha Coolidge should be expecting any nominations come awards time, but as a piece of fluffy entertainment, it goes down painlessly enough."

It seemed like Hilary's acting career was headed in the wrong direction. One reason for this was that she was always playing the same kinds of characters: nice girls. Hollywood producers seemed to have a hard time seeing beyond Hilary's good-girl **persona**, and she was not offered parts that were unusual or that would allow her to test herself as an actor. Hilary commented:

> "It always shocks me the lack of openness, the lack of imagination that some casting directors have. I would read a script and be so in love with that, and someone would be like, 'Hilary Duff? Oh, no, we don't want her for that.'"

Moving Forward 47

Haylie joined Hilary in the 2006 film *Material Girls*, which was poorly received by both fans and critics. "There is no edge to the movie at all, and that blandness will render it forgettable to anyone over the age of 12 or so, but for all that, it is pleasant enough, and occasionally even fun," wrote Pam Grady of Reel.com.

Dealing with a Stalker

The negative publicity surrounding *Material Girls* and her problems in getting good parts were bad enough. Hilary soon had a much more serious matter to deal with. She learned that an 18-year-old man was stalking her.

A member of the paparazzi snapped this photo of Hilary walking down a street in New York City. During 2006 Hilary had to deal with an obsessed fan who was stalking her and sent a threatening message to her boyfriend. The stalker was arrested in November 2006, and in January 2007 he was sentenced to four months in prison.

Moving Forward

Hilary had been long exposed to bizarre behavior from her fans. One time four young girls followed her into a restroom and put their ears against the wall of the stall Hilary was using. On another occasion, a male fan showed up at a concert wearing a hot dog costume and tried to catch her attention. Hilary once noted that:

> "It's still a little weird getting out of a car and having all these people screaming for you. Sometimes I get down thinking I don't have a normal life. I don't have any privacy."

This situation was different. The young man claimed that he had come to the United States from his native Russia because he loved Hilary, and threatened to eliminate anyone who kept the two of them apart—including Hilary's boyfriend Joel Madden. Things got so bad that Hilary had to obtain a **restraining order**. Eventually the man was arrested and sentenced to several months in jail.

Going to War

Hilary found some relief from an unexpected source. Noted actor John Cusack had written a film called *War, Inc.*, in which he would play a hit man assigned to kill an important government official in a fictitious Middle Eastern country. As part of the hit man's cover, he arranges a wedding involving a Russian pop star named Yonica. Cusack had written the part of the pop star with Hilary in mind.

When Hilary's agent called her with the news that Cusack wanted her, she was thrilled—until she learned that Yonica was a pop singer. That sounded too much like other roles she had played, and she wanted something different. Her agent urged Hilary to read the script. When she did, Hilary realized that it was a great part, and an opportunity to finally put her good girl image behind her. Nevertheless, she had doubts, which she expressed to Jennifer Vineyard of *MTV Movie News*:

> "It's off the wall and nuts and really smart and controversial. . . . And I was so excited about it, like, 'Gosh, can I do this? I don't know if I can do this!' Because you know what, when people won't take a chance on you, you have like no confidence."

Embracing Discomfort

No one would confuse *War, Inc.* with *Cheaper by the Dozen*, *The Perfect Man*, *Material Girls* or anything else Hilary had done before. The movie is a dark political **satire** about people trying to profit from a war in the Middle East. Hilary had to take on a completely different personality: with her jet-black hair, heavy makeup, and sexy clothing Yonica was about as far away from Lizzie McGuire as Hilary could get. She had to learn to speak with a Russian accent. She had to become comfortable handling a machine gun. She even had to spend several weeks on location in Bulgaria during the fall of 2006.

Cusack was pleased with Hilary's performance. "She's great," he said. "We had a great time, and she rocks in the film." He was so happy that he asked Hilary to do another serious film with him. Called *Talking with Dog*, it portrays a grim futuristic world scarred by global warming and other environmental catastrophes. She began working on *Talking with Dog* in 2007, and the film is expected to be released in 2008.

Breaking Up

In late 2006 Hilary experienced several disappointments in her personal life. First, she and boyfriend Joel Madden broke up after two and a half years. Compounding her pain, Joel almost immediately moved into a new relationship with Nicole Richie. Then, she learned that her father had started a relationship with another woman, and that her parents had decided to get a divorce after 22 years of marriage. In early 2007 Hilary told Elysa Gardner of *USA Today*:

> "For some reason, I was embarrassed that my family wasn't perfect . . . that some woman had broken it up."

She incorporated her feelings into the songs on her new album, *Dignity*, which was released in April 2007. She and Haylie collaborated on one track, "Gypsy Woman," which is about her father's extramarital affair. That was not the only song that referenced the split. Hilary said:

> "'Stranger' is a song I wrote about how my mom must feel around my dad. I made it seem like it was about a relationship I was in, because I didn't want people to know about my parents. But I've realized that so many people can relate to what I've gone through."

Moving Forward

Dignity offered a more mature sound than Hilary's earlier albums, and music critics responded favorably. She wrote all of the songs on the album, and in an interview Hilary admitted that "a lot of the songs on the record are obviously about [Joel Madden and their breakup] because I dated him for 2-1/2 years."

Dealing with *Dignity*

Dignity debuted at number three on the *Billboard* album chart. Although it has not sold as quickly as Hilary's other albums, *Dignity* did receive excellent reviews. Many critics commented on the way she had matured musically. "Duff set out to make an adult dance-pop record, with surprisingly successful results," wrote Andy Greene of *Rolling Stone*. *All Music Guide*'s Stephen Erlewine added:

> "Even if it's hard not to wish Hilary sounded closer to her age, with this small voice she still sounds relatable and, most of all, likable—perceptions that are only enhanced by her determined desire to hold onto her dignity in this tabloid age. She may still be caught between childhood and womanhood, but on *Dignity* she makes some serious headway into turning into a mature recording artist, which makes this an effective, strangely endearing album."

Reaching Out

Hilary's personal turmoil did not keep her from continuing to try to help others. She had not forgotten the suffering caused by Hurricane Katrina, and returned to the stricken city of New Orleans on the first anniversary of the disaster in August 2006. In early December 2006 she donated 200,000 meals to the survivors through USA Harvest. Stan Curtis, the organization's chairman said:

> "Hilary has set an extraordinary example with her generous contributions to the Gulf Coast victims of last year's tragic hurricanes. With her current contribution, Hilary will have donated over 2.7 million meals to the victims who still need these generous donations."

Nor would the personal turmoil keep her from advancing her acting career. In addition to *War, Inc.*, her 2007 movie releases included an animated comedy called *Foodfight!* It takes place in a supermarket after it closes for the night and the products come to life. As Sunshine Goodness, Hilary helps foil a plot to take over the market. Some of the other celebrities who lent their voices to the

Moving Forward

In August 2006 Hilary served meals during her visit to Camp Hope, Louisiana, a home for volunteers working to clean up the devastation of Hurricane Katrina. Hilary has donated a great deal of money to help victims of the storm. USA Harvest founder Stan Curtis calls her efforts "evidence of her wonderful leadership and caring about others."

animated comedy were Eva Longoria, Charlie Sheen, Wayne Brady, Christopher Lloyd, Chris Kattan, and Hilary's sister Haylie.

Continuing to Grow

In an interview with Lori Berger of *CosmoGIRL!*, Hilary said, "My whole life, parents of my fans have been coming up to me and saying, 'Hilary, we love you so much. Please, never change.'" Obviously, that is an impossible request—change is an important part of growing up and becoming an adult. Hilary's life has gone through several transformations over the past few years. She admits that she is looking forward to even more changes in the future:

54 HILARY DUFF

In 2007 Hilary spoke with *USA Today* about her future: "I want to be married and have kids, definitely, but not any time soon. A lot of things in my life have come faster than they do for most people.... I think that I'm still very normal, outside my un-normal life."

Moving Forward   55

> "I'm so excited about the possibilities ahead—but I'm also scared. I get sad and confused and question who I am and feel unsure about what I should do. But those are just growing pains, and something good will come out of them . . . everything will turn out okay."

On several occasions, Hilary has said that her life is like a fairy tale. But her success is firmly grounded in her hard work and determination. There is no doubt that she will continue to transform her career in ways that her fans can only imagine.

CHRONOLOGY

1987 Hilary Erhard Duff is born on September 28 in Houston, Texas.

1993 Appears in *Nutcracker* ballet.

1997 Appears in television movie *True Women*.

1998 Has title role in *Casper Meets Wendy*.

1999 Appears in *Soul Collector*.

Nominated for Young Artist Award for *Casper Meets Wendy*.

2000 Cast in *Daddio* but then dropped.

Cast in title role in *Lizzie McGuire*.

Wins Young Artist Award for *Soul Collector*.

2001 *Lizzie McGuire* debuts on January 19 and makes Hilary famous.

2002 Stars in Disney television feature *Cadet Kelly*.

2003 Makes feature film debut in *Agent Cody Banks*.

Stars in *Lizzie McGuire Movie*.

Ends contract with Disney.

Releases album *Metamorphosis*.

Releases single "So Yesterday".

Appears in *Cheaper by the Dozen*.

2004 Stars in *A Cinderella Story*.

Stars in *Raise Your Voice*.

Releases album *Hilary Duff*.

Begins dating Joel Madden.

2005 Appears in *The Perfect Man*.

Appears in *Cheaper by the Dozen 2*.

Releases album *Most Wanted*.

CHRONOLOGY

2006 Costars in *Material Girls* with sister Haylie.

Harassed by stalker.

Breaks up with Joel Madden.

2007 Appears in *War, Inc.*

Appears in *Foodfight!*.

Releases album *Dignity*.

ACCOMPLISHMENTS & AWARDS

Films
1997 *True Women* (made for TV)
1998 *Casper Meets Wendy*
1999 *The Soul Collector* (made for TV)
2001 *Human Nature*
2002 *Cadet Kelly* (made for TV)
2003 *Agent Cody Banks*
The Lizzie McGuire Movie
Cheaper by the Dozen
2004 *A Cinderella Story*
Raise Your Voice
2005 *The Perfect Man*
Cheaper by the Dozen 2
2006 *Material Girls*
2007 *War, Inc.*
Foodfight!
2008 *Talking with Dog*

Albums
2003 *Metamorphosis*
2004 *Hilary Duff*
2005 *Most Wanted*
2007 *Dignity*

Awards and Recognition
1999 Nominated, Young Artist Award, Best Performance in a TV Movie/Pilot/Mini-Series or Series—Young Actress Age Ten or Under

2000 Won, Young Artist Award, Best Performance in a TV Movie or Pilot—Supporting Young Actress

2002 Nominated, Kids' Choice Awards, Favorite Television Actress

Nominated, Young Artist Award, Best Performance in a TV Comedy Series—Leading Young Actress and Best Ensemble in a TV Series (Comedy or Drama)

2003 Won, Teen Choice Award, Choice Movie Breakout Star—Female

ACCOMPLISHMENTS & AWARDS

Nominated, Teen Choice Award, Choice Movie Actress—Comedy and Choice TV Actress—Comedy

Nominated, Kids' Choice Awards, Favorite Television Actress

Nominated, Young Artist Award, Best Ensemble in a TV Series (Comedy or Drama)

Fort Myers Beach Film Festival Rising Star Award

2004 Won, World Music Awards, Best New Female Artist

Won, Young Artist Award, Best Young Ensemble in a Feature Film

Won, Kids' Choice Awards, Favorite Female Singer;

Nominated, Kids' Choice Awards, Favorite Television Actress

Nominated, Juno Awards, Best International Album of the Year

Nominated, Teen Choice Award, Choice Movie Blush

2005 Won, Teen Choice Award, Choice Movie Blush Scene

Nominated, Teen Choice Award, Choice Movie Actress—Comedy, Choice Movie Chemistry, Choice Movie Liplock, and Choice Movie Love Scene

Won, Kids' Choice Awards, Favorite Movie Actress

Nominated, Kids' Choice Awards, Favorite Television Actress

2006 Nominated, Teen Choice Award, Choice Actress—Comedy

FURTHER READING & INTERNET RESOURCES

Books

Boone, Mary. *Hilary Duff.* Chicago: Triumph Books, 2003.

Brereton, Erin. *Hilary Rocks!* Chicago: Triumph Books, 2004.

Krulik, Nancy. *Hilary Duff: A Not-so-Typical Teen.* New York: Simon Spotlight, 2003.

Rappaport, Jill, and Wendy Wilkinson. *People We Know, Horses They Love.* Emmaus, Pa.: Rodale Books, 2004.

Rettenmund, Matthew. *Hilary Duff: All Access.* New York: Berkley Boulevard Books, 2005.

Web Sites

http://www.hilaryduff.com
Hilary Duff's official Web site includes information about her albums and films. Visitors can also join her official fan club and read Hilary's thoughts on her blog.

http://oh-hilary.com/#
The fan site OH-Hilary.com bills itself as the "number one source for everything and anything Hillary Duff." It includes links to news articles and photos.

http://www.people.com/people/hilary_duff/biography
This *People* magazine timeline of Hilary's life and career includes links to numerous articles about her that have appeared in the magazine over the years.

http://www.hilaryontheweb.com/interviews/hilary-duff-interviews-index.html
This page provides links to 14 interviews that Hilary has conducted with a number of different newspapers.

http://www.hduff.net/hilary/lizziemcguireepisodeguideseason1.htm
http://www.hduff.net/hilary/lizziemcguireepisodeguideseason2.htm
These pages provide summaries of each of the 65 episodes of *Lizzie McGuire*, as well as little-known information about the show.

GLOSSARY

audition—a tryout for a part in a play or musical performance.

callback—a request for an actor to return for further auditions.

charisma—a high degree of charm and appeal; personal magnetism.

demographic—a target market.

impetus—stimulus, pushing something into motion.

marquee—sign over a theater with the names of featured performers; also, the name recognition associated with featured performers.

persona—the public image that a notable individual tries to project.

pilot—television show produced as a sample of a proposed series. If network executives like the pilot, they typically order additional episodes.

platinum—designation given to a record that sells more than a million copies.

rehash—to present something again without making significant changes.

remixes—recordings that are changed by adding new material or rearranging certain elements.

restraining order—a court order that requires a particular person to stay away from someone else.

satire—the use of irony and sarcasm to criticize or make fun of actual human behaviors.

stereotype—an oversimplified image or idea about a person or group of people.

syndication—the sale of a television program that has already been broadcast to independent stations, so that it can be seen in reruns.

tsunami—an immense sea wave, usually generated by a volcanic eruption, that causes death and destruction when it comes ashore.

tween—a name for young people between the ages of eight and 12; preteen.

INDEX

Addams Family Reunion (film), 8
Agent Cody Banks (film), 23–24, 25
American Music Awards, 31

Barker, Lynn, 14, 24, 34
Bell, Josh, 24
Benedetti, Winda, 34
Berger, Lori, 37, 53
birth and childhood, 7–8, 13–16

Cadet Kelly (TV movie), 20
Carradine, Robert, 19
Carter, Aaron, 20, 26–27
Casper Meets Wendy (film), 8–9
charity work, 40, 42–43, 52–53
Cheaper By the Dozen (film), 25–26
Cheaper by the Dozen 2 (film), 43
Chiklis, Michael, 11
Churnin, Nancy, 40
A Cinderella Story (film), 34, 35, 38
Corbett, John, 37
Cordova, Randy, 43
Curtis, Sam, 52–53
Cusack, John, 49–50

Daddio (TV show), 10–11
dating. *See* romantic relationships
Delapa, Thomas, 34
Dignity (album), 44, 50–52
Duerden, Nick, 35
Duff, Haylie (sister), 7–8, 13, 16, 21, 42, 46–47
    friendship of, with Hilary, 14, 15
Duff, Hilary
    awards won by, 9, 25, 34
    birth and childhood, 7–8, 13–16
    box office record, 24, 25, 35, 38, 40, 43, 46
    charity work, 40, 42–43, 52–53
    clothing line, 33–34, 39
    critical reception of, 20, 24–25, 31, 34, 37, 38, 40, 43, 46, 52
    early roles, 8–11, 14–17
    earnings, 45
    feud of, with Lindsay Lohan, 26–27
    film career, 23–27, 34–35, 37–38, 40, 43, 46–47, 49–50, 52–53
    friendship of, with Haylie, 14, 15
    on *Lizzie McGuire*, 6, 10, 11, 16–22
    in *The Lizzie McGuire Movie* (film), 17, 24–25, 26
    romantic relationships, 20, 26–27, 35–37, 50, 51
    singing career, 27–31, 37, 40, 41, 50–52
    stalker of, 48–49
Duff, Robert "Bob" (father), 8, 16, 50
Duff, Susan (mother), 8, 16, 21, 46, 50

Erlewine, Stephen Thomas, 31, 37, 52

Foodfight! (film), 52–53

Gardner, Elysa, 50
Gates, Anita, 37, 38
Gillespie, Eleanor Ringel, 24–25
Girardi, Laura, 19
Grady, Pam, 46, 47
Greene, Andy, 52

Hanley, Tyler, 34
Hilary Duff: All Access Pass (DVD), 29
Hilary Duff (album), 37
Hope (TV movie), 8, 15
Human Nature (film), 9–10
Hunt, Bonnie, 26
Hunt, Jim, 26

INDEX

James, LeBron, 45

Kids' Choice Awards, 34
Kids with a Cause (charity), 40, 42
Kutcher, Ashton, 26

Lamberg, Adam, 19
Lance Armstrong Foundation (charity), 43
Landers, Jay, 28
Lizzie McGuire (TV show), 6, 10, 11, 16–22
The Lizzie McGuire Movie (film), 17, 24–25, 26
Locklear, Heather, 38
Lohan, Lindsay, 16, 26–27
Lurio, Eric, 46

Madden, Benji, 40
Madden, Joel, 35–37, 40, 49, 50, 51
Mansfield, Brian, 31
Martin, Steve, 26
Material Girls (film), 46–47
Metamorphosis (album), 28, 30–31, 34, 37
Monaghan, John, 34
Most Wanted (album), 40, 41
Muniz, Frankie, 23–24, 25
Murray, Chad Michael, 34, 35

Noh, David, 24

O'Regan, Seamus, 28

Paxton, Sara, 16
The Perfect Man (film), 38, 40

Raise Your Voice (film), 37–38
Rappaport, Jill, 13–14
Recke, Andre, 28
Return to Freedom (charity), 43
Richie, Nicole, 50
Rogow, Stan, 10, 16–17
romantic relationships, 20, 26–27, 35–37, 50, 51
Rosen, Craig, 27–28
Ross, Rich, 17
Roten, Robert, 24

Santa Claus Lane (album), 28
Shuster, Fred, 16–17
Soul Collector (TV movie), 9
Stroup, Kate, 16
Stuff by Hilary Duff (clothing line), 33–34, 39

Talking with Dog (film), 50
Teen Choice Awards, 25
Thomas, Jake, 19
Todd, Hallie, 19
Toy Mountain Campaign (charity), 43
True Women (TV movie), 8, 15

The Underworld (TV show), 8
USA Harvest (charity), 43, 52–53

Vergara-Paras, Lalaine, 19
Vineyard, Jennifer, 49

Wallace, Aaron, 20
War, Inc. (film), 44, 49–50, 52
What's Lizzie Thinking. See Lizzie McGuire (TV show)
Wilkinson, Wendy, 13–14

ABOUT THE AUTHOR

Jim Whiting has written nearly 100 books for young people and edited another 150. He has also published a monthly regional running magazine, served as sports editor for his local newspaper, written scores of freelance magazine and newspaper articles, advised an award-winning high school newspaper, taken photos and written event and venue descriptions for America Online, and acted as official photographer for the Antarctica Marathon. He lives in Washington state with his wife, Catherine.

Picture Credits

page

2: Newswire Photo/KRT
6: Photolink/FPS
9: iPhoto
10: Disney Channel/KRT
12: Disney Channel/KRT
15: Newswire Photo/NMI
17: Newswire Photo/NMI
18: Disney Channel/KRT
21: Newswire Photo Service
22: KRT/MCT
25: MGM/NMI
26: Walt Disney Pictures/NMI
27: New Millennium Images
29: StarMax
30: New Millennium Images
32: Fashion Wire Daily
35: Warner Bros. Pictures/NMI
36: BlackStar/PPP
38: New Line Cinema/MCT
39: Newswire Photo/NMI
41: UPI Newspictures
42: American Forces Press
44: WireImage Entertainment
47: Fashion Wire Daily
48: StarMax/PPP
51: Ace Pictures
53: DB2/WENN
54: Fashion Wire Daily

Front cover: AdverMedia Photos
Back cover: Walt Disney Pictures/NMI